MERAKI

A COLLECTION OF POEMS, SHORT STORIES AND MONOLOGUES

MS MEENAKSHI

To all the procrastinators,

Who are definately getting somewhere.

Contents

Contents

Acknowledgements

I'd like to thank my entire family for being extremely supportive of my unhinged decisions, my brother for putting up with long periods of awkward silence when he asked about how my book was going, my parents for painstakingly searching for ways to get this done, and my friends for being constant inspirations and scapegoats for my writing.

From the bottom of my soul, thank you.

Preface

I didn't prepare myself mentally to write this, so I'll keep it short.

This wasn't exactly what I had in mind when I decided I wanted to write a book. I had a brilliant plot for a super long novel, a character profile, and a draft with the most plot holes ever seen.

However, that document got deleted by accident. Oops.

So, here's a collection of some of the short stories, poems and monolouges I've written over the course of about 2 or 3 years. The ones not included are either too embarrassing, too long, or contain lore that is far too complicated for me to process and put into words.

With that being said, have fun reading!

1. Finding a Lost cause

An exasperated cry rang out through the lush green fields. He was with her just this morning. How far could someone go within a span of three hours? A lot, in her twin's case. Feeling that she'd rested enough, the young girl set off yet again, searching desperately for her beloved twin.

She tried asking the neighbours, who were confused as to why she was asking. "Poor thing, she's going mad" They whispered, which only added to her confusion. They all knew she had a twin, so why was this any different? Twins aren't always together, are they? They did fight, and get separated from time to time, but he always came back to her, and she was never too far. They promised each other that. And yet, he doesn't come back to her. So, she tries to reach out to him. It's not part of the promise, and she's not very happy about that, but she can get back at him all she wants once she finds him. He was the older twin after all.

Confused, frustrated, and worried, she ran aimlessly, paying no heed to where she was going, until her foot collided with a huge shell. A pretty one, she hated to admit, pure white with violet edged shining in the dim twilight sun. She froze. Violet was her favourite colour. Only he knew that. Bingo. "I found you! So, stop hiding!"

Minutes passed by in silence. Black dots obscured her vision. When she could see clearly again, it hit her like a truck and a brick wall combined together. Her twin went far away from the fields a year ago. She didn't know if he would come back, and she was just too far this time.

Still, she plops down on the grass, chin resting on her palm as she tilts her head inquisitively. "So. When are you going to come back?"

Above, the statue of the soldier smiled down at her, unmoving, lifeless.

2. A mother's lament

Every year there's a whole lot more,
I don't think I can take it any longer
I just want to kick them out the door.
Oh, but how can I?
They are my children after all,
I cannot find the heart to leave them to die.
So let them live their dangerous ways,
Let them trample me, choke me, destroy me,
But I love them, no matter what anybody says.

3. A mother's lament: Afterword

The woman runs, afraid for her future.

Don't look back.

Don't look back.

Don't-

And then she sees it.

Kneeling down pitifully are her children, the ones she brought into this life, and the ones who will be buried deep inside her after they pass.

Kneeling down pitifully are her children, who she's brought up with her very hands, chased playfully with the very legs she uses to run away.

Their once bright eyes are gaunt, devoid of life, yet so sad.

Come back, mother.

Please don't leave us.

Come back mother.

Tears pool in her eyes. How daft must she have been to think of doing such a thing to her children? How could she have ever left them to die like this?

She turns and darts back toward her beloved children. She couldn't stand the sight of them destroying themselves, choking and sputtering, short on breath.

With her gone, they wouldn't last an hour.

So she runs back to them, pours the air back into their shrivelled up lungs, wipes the tears off their faces, and embraces them all in her green arms.

Years later, she smiles at them all through her pain. Her beautiful, smart children, all grown up and successful, going about their lives.

So, she smiles, despite the browns and greys covering her lush green body.

4. First, never last

The oldest child is the spoilt one, pampered with the best of
riches
The oldest child gets all that is pretty and new
The oldest child is always loved first
The oldest child knows of true horrors, only few.
The oldest child is one who smiles most,
The one whose tears are never seen
The leader, the genius, the prodigy,
And yet they are the child who's hopelessly lost
The oldest child, the fairest of them all,
Yet remains to believe themselves a monster
Who doesn't see themselves worthy of humanity
The presumed angels that have long since had their fall
The oldest child is the one forced to grow up too fast
The oldest child is the one far too observant for their own
good
The oldest one is one who hears too much
The oldest child is the one to eat the last
The oldest child is a strange one yet,
With their mother's rage and father's grief
It leaves no space for worries of their own
But what can the fish do trapped within it's net?

5. Wisps of a past

Hot breeze blows through the courtyard
Laughter bubbles through the tall buildings
I watch the older ones like me I hold high in regard
Together in groups near the big tree, sitting.
The bell is loud but a welcome grace
And I race my friends to the library,
Our one true escape, our special place
The books on the shelves twinkling with vibrancy.
I hear screams of joy and laughter outside,
I see the children playing in the huge ground
Winning races that makes them swell with pride
It reminds me of when my old friends were still around.
I pick a book and I look around
It finally, finally sinks in
This is, perhaps the last time I stand on these grounds
The thought makes hair stand on my skin.
Thirteen years of joy, of sorrow,
Thirteen years of annoyance, of anger,
Thirteen years of "I'll do it tomorrow",
Thirteen years of endless chatter.
In a few months it's time for goodbyes,
I don't think I'm ready just yet
I haven't made enough excuses, enough lies,

But what you want, you don't always get.
Soon they will be gone
And I will be left behind all alone,
With only memories of them all,
To allow me to finally move on.

6. I have a friend

I have a friend see,
One who's as funny as can be,
And he says an awful lot
About words that rhyme
And words that do not
This funny fellow often says,
That the word chocolate,
And the word lead,
''they rhyme mate!''
In his opinion I hear,
The word saw
Rhymes with haw
I don't know if I should tell him,
That haw is the fruit the Hawthorne bears,
And not what he expects it to mean.
And yet this funny friend of mine,
His funny poetic lines,
His claims that rap music could be a poet's call,
His ridiculous statements,
Sometimes don't sound bad after all

7. Anomaly

"So you're dead?"

"Yup."

"You're joking."

She expected the day to go about dully, as usual, like clockwork. She did not expect to meet a dead person.

Some say that would be a ghost.

Ghosts don't appear in front of bored people. Do they?

All was well(or as well as it could be) that morning when she bumped into someone in the empty abandoned storeroom.

"What the-"

"Hi."

She stares at the guy for a full minute. "Sorry who-"

"Are you dead too?"

"No, why would I be?"

"I assumed this was the afterlife."

"It's not. It's a storeroom in a school."

"Oh."

And he just decides to follow her around for the rest of the day. She lets him, because she can think of nothing more. It wasn't all that different from a normal day, yet it felt somewhat.... Nice.

When he follows her home too, however, she stops to ask him questions, because it was about time.

"So you're dead?"

"Yup."

"You're joking"

"Nope"

"How can I see you if you're dead?"

He shrugs, and she pokes his arm. Solid. He's not a ghost then.

Her parents do not see the boy. He is as surprised as she is, so there was no point in getting any answers out of him.

"They can't see me?"

"Oh come on, I thought you'd know why"

"Well, er, I don't."

She sighs. "Are you planning to stick with me forever?"

"Depends on how long you believe forever to be"

She shrugs. "A year, maybe more."

He raises an eyebrow questioningly.

She frowns. She couldn't possibly tell him the truth, it was far too embarrassing. She'd just have to come up with another reason.

"Well in a little over a year, I'll move up another grade and then I'll graduate. That's my forever."

"Why?"

"Because, well, it'll be the start of another beginning. So after I graduate there would be another forever." It wasn't a lie, but it wasn't the complete truth either.

"That's an odd way of thinking."

Another shrug.

Silence.

It's the same kind of silence that fills her room every day, but it somehow felt different. Slightly comforting. Maybe it was the sounds of another human being, of shuffling around, of steady breaths, of knuckles cracking. And then she remembers.

"Hey."

He looks up.

"Since you're staying forever, don't you want to know my name?"

A nod.

"My name's Hira. "

"I'm Asim."

"Well it's nice to meet you Asim"

He grins.

She grins back.

8. True 'Peace'

The breeze flows slightly, ruffling my hair.

"You seem fatigued." The voice is soft and melodic. "I am." I answer, not bothering to glance back. "Pray tell, why are you here, of all places, at such an odd hour?"

"To rest."

"And why would you want to rest in such a place?"

"A rather ignorant question, dear acquaintance. Do you not see the beauty of this place?"

"I am afraid I cannot. Do tell, fair maiden, why you find this place beautiful?"

"The lush green trees and pretty peonies shine in the moonlight that smiles down at us. The river, which roars in all its fury during the day, is flowing peacefully, nestling the dew decorated lotus petals. It's silent, it's peaceful."

"I see. I can picture it in my mind's eye now".

Naturally, I was curious. Someone who couldn't see?

"Well, what do you see?"

"Would you like me to show you?"

Now I contemplate. It seems like something only she can see, and I suppose curiosity got the best of me.

And I'm glad it did.

"Show me."

Soft, gentle, tinkling laughter filled the air as she did just that, as warm liquid flowed down my cheeks, showing me a sight I would never forget, making me feel at absolute peace at last.

Many years later

A tall, slender girl watches from a distance as a boy settles down on the grass, the wind ruffling his hair slightly.

She approaches him, asking the same questions she was once asked. The answers were the same. Smiling, she asked him "Would you like me to show you?"

"Show me."

And that she did once again, passing on the sight to him as the same warm liquid, of the colour she adored flowed down his cheeks , in hopes that the entire world would soon be brought to peace.

And to date, the villagers warn their people not to wander out too far in the night, in fear that they might be taken away. Taken away to be shown 'peace'.

9. A kind of 'home'

Objects clattered across the ground as a pale black-haired girl hurried to pick them up. This part of the city was abandoned, for now at least. It wasn't long before someone would find the place. And she hadn't encountered a single human in the past 6 months (she chose not to) and was glad she hadn't.

She just had to think about it because an hour later, she was on the hunt for another abandoned building, but this time with an obnoxious tufted titmouse (In her defence, her companion did look like one), who wouldn't stop talking. "Listen. I am not thinking about attracting attention or meeting up with someone or looking for another crack headed idiot to deal with so will you please shut it?"

"Alright alright. As you say your majesty. Say doesn't that look good? We're miles away from the other city and it doesn't seem like anyone will come here for a while." She hummed, slowly opening the door to the empty shop. It wasn't in a particularly bad condition except for toppled over chairs and broken shelves. Compared to the others, not a huge amount of damage. Her train of thoughts were interrupted with a "Hey it's a candy store! Just our luck!" "Is there any food left?" "Loads. No one's been here yet! We should totally crash here for a few days." "We'll see. For now, we should focus on storing as much as we can. You have a bag or something?"

"Of course I have one. And it has loads of free space." "Get collecting then."

As it got darker, she decided that she'd take the first watch. "You sure?" "Yeah. Sleep doesn't come all that easy to me anyway." And now, she realized how much she missed being able to rest completely, without a care in the world. It was strange how her companion trusted her so much. She was either a complete idiot, oblivious to the current situation, or that she had a plan in mind and seems to be playing dumb. Either way, she had to be careful.

But still, she hated to admit that it was somewhat of a relief that she had company, even if it was someone annoying and loud. Sighing, she stared out the glass panes of the once colourful candy shop, looking at the peaceful night sky. She'd always found peace in looking at the dull navy colour, sometimes sprinkled with a sparkling dot of white. White reminded her of what she left behind, so she avoided looking at it. But now, she couldn't look away. The stars were enticing, pulling her gaze towards them, and she didn't dare resist or avert her gaze, even as warm tears streamed down her face. She'd felt something. Something she never felt before. It burned, and bristled in her, and her throat was constricted, making breathing difficult. Her eyes burned. This, she realized, was guilt. Funnily enough, it took her 8 entire months and human interaction to realize what she'd done. She abandoned her family, left them to rot, and had runaway without a care. Just as she was about to wipe her eyes with her sleeve, she felt a hand brush against hers. "It's okay. You didn't do anything wrong. You tried to save yourself, and that's not selfish at all. So come on, wipe those tears away, and run away with me. We can get through this hell together."

"To the end of the line?"

"Right to the very end."

And when morning comes, they scout for another place all over again, no matter how much it hurt to leave the past behind.

10. Yours truly, nobody

Stay away from such people he said,
They're crooks and cheats,
Don't let them get to your head.
But my good man you see,
Your lass is just like them,
A crook and cheat like me.
She and I, we're the same,
We're angry foolish children,
Playing life like a game.
She doesn't understand love like you do
And neither do I,
But she has someone she writes letters to.
These letters I come to know,
Are not to a lover or a friend,
But to herself, like a fatal blow.
She has so much she wishes to say,
And so much she keeps in her head,
It keeps her up night and day.

11. Four little ducks

Four little ducks in a little blue pond,
Mama duck ran away
Papa duck is nowhere to be found.
Four little ducks waddle too far,
Oh! There's something speeding by
I hear a splat and the screech of a car.
Four little ducks now ducks no more,
Papa duck, Mama duck, where are you?
I see a man in black open the door.
Four little ducks disappear behind that door,
Leaving four little red puddles behind
I watch as the guilty driver is shook to the core.
Four little ducks now ducks again,
No longer yellow but pure snow white,
Here their new life begins.

12. A soldiers final say

"I should've never signed that paper.

I thought I was serving my country, protecting my 'brothers and sisters'.

Huh, what a joke.

I still wake at the crack of dawn, expecting to be rallied out to the grounds.

I still perk up to the slightest of sounds, expecting an ambush or a figure in the dark.

I still flinch in fear when the fireworks go off.

I still feel the weight of the gun in my cold, empty hands.

I still hear the cries of agony of my comrades.

I still see the light fade from my enemies eyes.

Enemy? What a cruel word. Because in the end, weren't we all humans?

No. No.... we were puppets. Lifeless, pawn like puppets designed to dance to the tune of our cruel puppeteers, thrown away like rag dolls when we were no longer needed.

When will this stop? When will they wake up? The worst is done for now... but it will repeat again and again in a wretched cycle.

So please, please, let this suffering stop. "

13. One side to a story

The girl looked across to the class president, craning her neck to get a better view of such a popular 'role model', hidden amongst her large group of friends, all vying for her attention, praising her, entertaining her.

She sighs.

She is writing her sloppy looking notes when she sees her walk towards the desk.

"Hey" She says sweetly. "Care to spare some time?" She looked up, eyes wide. The class president? "Um.. Sure" she mutters, unsure of what to feel.

The class president lead the way, as she always did, and the second best fool followed her, like she always did. " So,I saw your work in the school magazine. "

That monstrosity? She saw that? Red flooded her cheeks. "I just wanted to say…. It was brilliant. I adored it." A warm smile.

"What?" her voice was barely above a whisper.

The president raised a well poised eyebrow. "I said, your work was brilliant. I was thinking if we could publish it on one of the school boards."

The school board? Only the best work was accepted for such an honour. An honour she didn't deserve. "I- I couldn't possibly! It's only a feeble article I wrote on whim and-"

"Is it so difficult to believe that your article was good?" It was a rather innocent question, one without any malicious intent, but it set her on the edge anyway.

"Well…" Her voice shook, slightly "Not everyone has talent like yours or-"

"What does my talent have to do with anything? You have yours. Embrace it. You don't need anything else if you have your talent and passion. Clearly, you've done this a lot, and clearly, you're good at it."

"That may be so, but it's nothing special. Nothing that will get me very far. This… this kind of 'intelligence' you claim I have is just something every human being possesses. I'm nothing unique, or different."

"Why do you think that way?" she has the guts to ask.

"Because" the second best breathes out "Everyone loves only the smartest, the special one, the one with the best grades. Nobody- Nobody loves a stupid kid."

14. The ruthless cycle

Papers and papers all around
Not one pen to be found
Is that how her life will go on?
The leaves fall,
The trees wilt,
Hey! They closed down that mall.
It's colder than it was last year,
The sun hasn't come up in ages,
Even the sky isn't blue and clear.
There are new people she sees,
They're so large and scary,
But still, she sings to herself,
"One day spring it will be".
The guns go boom deep into the night
The people scream in agony, not knowing what's wrong, what's right
She is angry, but why?
Should she not run?
Should she not hide?
What is she doing,
Running out into the night?
She runs and runs until she can run no further
She hears the footsteps come closer

And closes her eyes, and she can open them no longer.

15. Anything with you

Home was distant, cold, with no one around. Sure school was loud but, it was better than anywhere else. It was a comforting type of loud, noises that didn't make her flinch all the time. Even if she never conversed with her classmates, they were kind, Maya was kind. And she liked it that way.

"Are you sure you don't want to come over this time?"

"Yes, I'll go with my parents."

"Alright, but you're always welcome to change your mind!"

A part of her hoped she'd be more persuasive, but oh well, she couldn't always rely on Maya. Besides, it was time she stopped running away from her aversion. They were to go on a holiday to the mountainside, a place she adored. The majestic, towering mountains, winding roads and long bus rides, gushing streams, olive green trees, juicy orange apricots, colourful flowers in vibrant shades and the cool refreshing winds that brushed across her face as she ducked her head out the window helped her forget the emptiness in the large villa. She was rudely jerked out of her pleasant daydream by the teacher. She'd always gaze down upon her with an unpleasant countenance, forever unsatisfied.

Despite all that, she had Maya, and she felt that was all she needed. As long as Maya was there by her side, she could do anything.

And then came parent teacher week. Her parents arrived along with everyone else's.

Maya found them in the gardens, taking a walk. From a distance, it would seem like they were perfect, happy even, but she knew what happened behind closed doors what others couldn't see.

Many assumed her best friend to be a snob, owing to her silent and distant demeanor.

Her parents did nothing to ease this rumour, but only added fuel to the fire with their expensive car and fancy packages they sent to her. And so people came to avoid her, hate her even, for something so empty as wealth and status.

They called Maya naive, some nicer ones called her a Saint, for being a friend of "Her royal highness". It never bothered her in the slightest, for she knew what she truly was like- Witty, creative, humorous and caring, just the type of person she'd want to be around. Her presence was comforting, quiet, serene. Now Maya adored noise, it was fun and never made her feel lonely, but the serenity about her was something she couldn't explain.

It was only natural she was shocked after finding out about her condition. It was a rather uncommon disorder, especially in this century, where human minds had developed a tenfold along with technology.

It wasn't like she was completely normal either. Despite looking completely healthy, Maya had a rare disease in her heart, which was a ticking time bomb so to say.

For the past few years, it had been a routine tradition that she'd joined Mayas family for the holidays, and she seemed to be happiest with them. That happiness went both ways she supposed. They were both embodiments of the sun to each other, brightening up one another's lives. But this time she was surprised to find that she had received word from her parents that she was to go with them on a trip to the mountains. Maya didn't fancy her friend's parents very much. She always sensed that there was something amiss about them, something cold and distant. Her friend always seemed to be closed off around them, mechanical even, and the formality between them made her flinch. Families were not meant to be formal, prim, and proper, were they?

16. If it ever happens

People often ask me,
A strange question indeed
That of I ever marry,
Who would it be?
So I think a moment and I say
Well I am quite the young lass,
And I haven't thought of it yet
But maybe a few years
And I'll find my way
And to this they ask
Do you not imagine?
And then I start to wonder
Is this something to ponder?
I imagine myself in a few years
Coming home from work
And at the dining table
A little note that says,
"Flowers for you, my dear"
Perhaps I smile a little, slightly lost
And breathe deeply the flowery scent,
Of the bouquet of bougainvilleas
I seem to love the most
Perhaps I share a late night chat,

With the person I call dear,
Maybe we'll have a pet or two
Or children if any I bear
So yes, I do wonder sometimes,
Of a life in the future, soon,
I don't think it goes that way though,
Unless I've been given a godly boon.

17. The power of the unknown

The young student sat, unsure of what his future had come to. He was pretty certain he's chosen a different path.

Well, it wasn't exactly his choice, if he was being honest. But he'd agreed to it, so it was practically his own decision to learn slice open human bodies for a living. Then again, it was either that or burying himself in deep numbers he couldn't possibly grasp. Shaking such thoughts away (he really has to start respecting his future profession soon) he gathered his books and placed them neatly on top of the desk. No odd angles, no messy positions, all ordered from largest at the bottom to smallest at the top. The desk next to him was quite contradictory. He blinked. How someone could fathom what lied there was beyond him. Papers scattered in all directions, pens and other stationary sprawled around and textbooks on the brink of falling. He felt he should help the student, as much as the sight hurt his eyes, and gently tapped his shoulder. He refused his offer for help, stating that he liked it better that way.

Having given up on making any sense out of that, he looked around at the students piling in. He felt that the way people arranged thier desks, defined them, somehow. And so far, today, he'd seen desks like his, desks with vibrant colours, desks with decorations, desks with food. Not to mention that he was still rather curious about his messy neighbour, who had been keeping up incessant chatter with other students the entire time. And right when he decides to talk to him, the teacher enters the room, silencing all of them in a heartbeat. Adults were forever a mystery to him, although he was to be one in about a year anyway.

He does get to talk to the messy student later on and finds that he's taking the same classes as he is. He realizes then that talking to him was not the best idea, because the messy student takes this as an open invitation to sit next to him in most classes. It takes a lot of effort to not let his gaze wander to the desk to his right the entire day.

It goes along well for the next few days, and he realizes he might actually like this messy student. As time passes, he comes to the slightly uncomfortable realization that he loves this messy student, but at the same time, has an irresistible urge to somehow get him out of his sight. This confuses him. Can you truly want to be far, far away from someone you love?

And one day, as they sit together in the late hours in the library, his hatred gets the better of him. As the messy student raises his head from his textbook, he's met with a little 'pop' and a pretty red dot on his forehead, chocolate bar still hanging limp from his mouth.

He smiles through his tears. Why was he crying?

Well either way, at long last, everything will be perfect again.

Probably.

18. Was it something wrong?

I destroyed someone's soul today,

Is that wrong?

I made them cry because of the things I say,

Am I wrong?

But it's fair is it not,

If they said such terrible things to me first,

If I was the one who was hurt a lot,

It's fair, is it not?

I know that words are a double edged sword,

That what I say might come back to haunt me

But why is it that they're the only one that's adored,

And I'm the one who has to flee?

I think I'll remember this now,

That every time I say something mean,

Know that it's not me who will have to bow,

But the person who hurt me.

19. (Un)Faithful Hope

Water dripped down onto the concrete ground from the grey rumbling clouds above. Rain.

The trio skipped down the path, the rain soaking up their shoes while they splash around in the puddles.

Innocent laughter filled the air along with the melodious splish splash of the water.

The oldest was the first to break the silence. "My parents say we have to move away soon."

The laughter stopped.

"What- What do you mean?"

"We have to go away. Far, far away."

"No!" the youngest cries out. "You can't leave us alone!"

"I know I know I don't want to!" she said, tears pooling in her eyes.

"Why do you have to go anyway?" The middle asks, tilting his head.

"I don't know.... My parents just said that we can't stay here any longer. That it's not safe."

"But-"

"I don't know, okay?! They were really serious about it."

"Okay..."

"Well then, promise you'll write and text loads and loads?"

"Yeah and that you'll never forget us!" The youngest piped up

The oldest smiled, wiping away her tears. "I promise."

And it was an unwritten rule that promises were never broken.

Months passed by. The two waited amidst the chaos crawling around the city, hearing nothing about their friend. The boy knew their parents knew something, but he never mentioned this to the younger.

Her questions, of course, were endless.

"Do you think she's forgotten us?"

He gives her a reassuring smile. "Of course not. She always keeps her promises. Just give her time."

Two teenagers sat on a blanket in the park, a plate of biscuits and a bottle of sprite between them. The younger broke the peaceful silence.

"It's been five whole years. Do you think she's ever coming back?"

The boy sighed.

"I don't know."

She hums in response, almost as if she expected the answer.

"Let's head back, shall we? It might rain soon" She said, her voice wavering slightly.

"I'm sure she's alright, she probably can't contact us" He makes an attempt at consolation.

"I try to think that, but considering the reason why she went away...."

"Her parents made an early decision, I'm sure they weren't hurt-"

"You don't know that!"

His eyes widen at her outburst.

"You're overthinking this. Come on, let's go home."

Ignoring the dread settling in his chest, he helps her pack the things up.

Another uneventful year passed by, but neither of them forgot her. He had given up all hope, assuming the worst. He hadn't told this to the younger, who was still hopeful of their friend's return.

Rain drizzled softly against the concrete ground. The sound of agitated voices filled the air, as her boots stomped into the puddles.

Both of them glared at each other and just as he opened his mouth to retort-

"Dear me, at each other's throats again?"

All three umbrellas fell to the ground with a splash as the three of them grinned with their eyes full of tears.

20. A bedtime story

"Ma!"

The exclamation brings out a bright smile on the stern accountant's face as she settles down on the little stool by her daughter's bed. "Sorry I'm late" she says gently. "Got held up by some meetings."

Her daughter only offers a smile, one that seems so wise, so ill fitting to her 11 year old countenance. "That's okay" She says quietly. "I had Smeagol to keep me company until now." She leans over to pat the head of the German shepherd perched by her feet, staring patiently at her. They sit in comfortable silence for a few moments. And then-

"Hey, ma?"

"Yes dear?"

"Are you too tired from work?"

Yes, she was

"Of course not. What's up?"

"Will you tell me a story?"

A story?

Her daughter hadn't asked for a story in years. What brought this on?

"I know, I know, it's not normal. But you haven't been late like this, not ever, so I was worried. I still am."

"Worried about what?" She didn't have to ask, she already knew the answer.

"Worried that one day you'll leave me behind."

Swallowing back the lump in her throat, she manages to smile in what she hopes a reassuring way.

"Even if the sun blows up, I would never."

It was their little joke, from a passage in an encyclopaedia that the sun would one day self destruct and they would all die. The two of them found it strangely hilarious and made it their joke ever since.

It cracks a little laugh out of her, before she begins to cough violently and her mother rushes to rub soothing circles on her back.

"Now will you tell me a story?" She whispers once she's calmed down.

"Of course. Once upon a time, long, long ago, there lived a princess-"

"Not that kind of story! Tell me something more.... Grown up"

"Grown up?"

"You know, like non fiction. Something not about childish things," she scrunches up her nose "like fairies and princesses and dragons or where everyone lives happily ever after"

Non fiction? She felt her heart sink. How did she grow up so fast? Just the other day she was reading about magic and wizards and now-

"I don't hate your stories ma! It's just.... I want to try something different today. So please will you tell me a grown up story?"

Because really, how could you say no to your daughter?

"Alright then, let me tell you a story, a real one. It- It doesn't have a happy ending though."

Her daughter smiles, and it feels ever so foreign. "Perfect"

"It's just like mine."

21. An ode to the heartless

It's 4AM

And your student's crying.

She's struggling, unable to comprehend your words.

And yet, you still sleep, uncaring.

She failed her test yesterday, rejected by your harsh glare.

Why was it not directed at anybody else? Why her?

She approached you for help after mustering up the courage she had.

Yet you pushed her away.

And now, with her parents livid, she has a heavy price to pay.

And I ask you, dear teacher,

Isn't that waht school is for? To ask questions? To learn, and to be provided with the facilities to do so, no matter what you can or cannot do?

She's falling deep into her misery, that you created. And yet, to you, it doesn't matter.

Oh, and I do hope you're aware of what happened the previous year.

I hope you remember that his blood is on your hands.

Why does it matter if she's different?

Have you truly given up on her just because she fails to grasp your words like the rest of us?

Is it because she's different? Is that so wrong?

It's 6AM.

You wake up to the sound of a thud and splatter.

You look down to find a pool of blood.

I hope you know, darling teacher, that her blood is on your hands too.

And it will never, ever wash off.

22. Apologies

She sighs.

Why had she begun to yell at him when he only suggested something that would help her study better? She too, was searching for an answer.

She figured she should at least start by apologizing, which was not her area of expertise. Still, she figured, she could try.

She starts big, with a sticky note. I think I'll try again.

She opens her textbook, and after staring at it for a few minutes, concentrates on the words written. She gets past the first few pages, before her thoughts begin to spiral, and soon she's daydreaming about her favourite book.

And soon, they all died, the winds of the city blowing through dust and smoke.

Hold on, that didn't make much sense. She frowned, and picked up a piece of paper.

The sights of death hung heavily in the dust and smoke ridden air of the city. The man in the long coat walked through the corpses, mourning the loss of his family, his friends, and all he holds dear, even those he has never met, all in the name of war.

She hums, satisfied, and pins the paper in her dairy. And then slaps her hand against her forehead. She was supposed to be doing her homework, dammnit, not doing something as profoundly idiotic as writing about war. Besides, she sighed to herself as she recalled the words of someone from a very long time ago, what would a young girl such as herself know about war? Sure, she had read books about it, but does that truly make her worthy enough to write about it?

Perhaps not.

She turns the page of her textbook once more and falls into the familiar routine of skimming through her notes and trying to remember what she'd read, but only in vain.

See she tried, she really did, but come what may, she couldn't quite remember what came next in the reactivity series, or what a particular formula would lead to. And every so often she'd relapse into day dreaming again, staring blankly into the white wall in front of her, which was suddenly a painting of several hues, a painting on which she could do anything.

Until reality came tumbling down on her shoulders like the largest boulder in the world, usually by loud voices across the hallway, or a doorbell or footsteps.

The sun has set by the time she finally completes her homework, and she realises she hasn't quite tried hard enough, as she meekly admits it to him.

The disappointment in his eyes hurts more than anything else. She was really bad at apologies, wasn't she?

23. A letter, written in the darkest of nights

To my dearest friend,
And a friend no more,
I thought time could stand still see,
But that, that was simply summer.
We danced, we laughed, we played around
Until it was nighttime, and in the dark,
I sat nursing my aching knee.
And now it's oh so different yes?
With you now a distant stranger,
Me, a hopeless loser,
Following you around everywhere
Someone who's never loved you less.
Tell me I'm wrong, please
Tell me that you still love me
Just as much as I love you
Even if it's a lie, tell me,
Because anything's worth your cruel tease.

24. Forget you not

People think me heartless sometimes I hear,
They say I don't seem feel much
That I'm quite the cruel child with too much to bear
And I have a just a little hunch
That what they say is the truth.
But you, oh you knew me,
You knew me more than anyone really
Even those who claimed to know me most,
You were always there when you needed to be,
To make sure I never got lost.
I'm lost now, and I don't know how to go back,
Far away from the place that's "home",
Please, please won't you help me?
Won't you tell me what I am? What I have?
Won't you tell me what I lack?
I didn't cry that night,
Or the nights after for years to come by,
I didn't speak about it either,
But I was still so, so scared,
That away those memories of you would fly.
I found some old things of yours like lucky charms,
A perfume and jewels that shone like you,
The jewels I don't keep, for I don't fancy any,

But the perfume I spritz when I'm feeling blue,
And I try to imagine the comforts of being in your arms.
And now it's been longer still,
I'm a little less lost and a lot wiser,
Because I catch glimpses of you paying a bill,
Sitting in that chair on your tab,
Lighting the lamp as you always did.

25. The escape from 'escape'

Cars screeched across the roads, ignoring the traffic signals and voices clamouring over the loudspeakers. People flood the streets, faces painted with worry.

In contrast to this, two teenagers stand absolutely still on the sidewalk, silently observing the chaos unfold.

"Do you reckon it's true? What they said in the news?"

"Must be. It would be pretty daft to pull a prank this huge." The green eyed one laughs.

Their parents were long gone, escaping to another continent as soon as they heard the news, leaving in quite the hurry, leaving most their possessions behind. The two of them however, chose to stay behind, promising their parents they would join them soon, much to their dismay.

"You think they'll miss us?" The boy asks, stealing a glance at the girl.

She scoffs. "Not a chance."

And that was that.

They walk across the road, heading to an abandoned library a few kilometres ahead. Taking advantage of the silence and absence of the strict librarian, they scour through the restricted section, giggling at the amount of dark magic novels that were contained there.

"You do know the city's probably going to blow up in the next few days?" She asks casually, sifting through a huge encyclopaedia.

"With all the evacuation announcements, how could I not?" He replies with a roll of his bright brown eyes.

She laughs at that, shaking her head in amusement.

And after a few moments of silence,

"And are you planning to do the same, *dear sir*?" her voice is lilting, mocking him.

"Depends on your decision, *darling*." He retorts.

Another half hour passes in comfortable silence and out of nowhere-

".....you're truly okay with this?"

"Of course." She says it like it's the most natural thing in the world.

"You might actually die, you know?"

"So might you."

"I know that, but you…"

"I truly don't mind."

He raises an eyebrow at this. He expected she was only following him around because of her loneliness. He figured she'd escape at the last moment, for he knew the notion of death wasn't agreeable with her.

She smiles. "It's better we live our happy little lives for the few days we have left. I can't imagine why people would give up everything they had for some unknown, uncertain future. We're going to die soon anyway, so we might as well die happy, right?"

He couldn't agree more.

26. How to be (not) a genius in 5 steps

The first step, would be to grow increasingly bored with how your life is going.

Aaloka knew this all too well. Being an only child *did* not help at all.

She decided she wanted a sibling, which was laughed off as a childish whim at the time. She huffed. Whatever. Adults were always thinking she was little and foolish.

The second step, is far more interesting. Stumble upon a book while raiding your father's very important bookshelf and become completely enamoured with it.

The second step would then lead to an unhealthy obsession with books of all kinds, though she explicitly preferred fantasical fairy tales.

Oh, and get a sibling on the way. Looks like parents actually took that request seriously. Oh well, it'd be a while before she'd have to deal with the baby, who looked far too peaceful and content with sleeping and crying all day to entertain her nagging.

The third step, would be to complete what's described as an 'inhumane' amount of books while watching your school grades take a short ride on the roller coaster.

The second she'd looked at her latest math test, where an unforgiving 'C-Grade' looked back at her, she knew she was done for.

So of course, she simply had to work a *little* bit harder, and she did. It made her parents proud, her teachers happy, her peers envious and admiring, on top of which she still got to read as much as she liked.

The only downside? She'd convinently forgotten to pick something other than reading to be good at.

So all she was at that moment was simply a voracious reader. Nothing more, nothing less.

So the fourth step would be to find another hobby, by which time she was already too old for the usual ones.

Aaloka should've given up by then, but she went ahead and tried to pursue a childhood dream of playing the violin.

She'd say it was going pretty well, for once.

The fifth and final step would be to try and completely alter her personality, fall into questionable company, get hurt, and find solace in a group of three girls who she's sure have a few screws lose.

Well it's not like she has all her braincells intact either. Plus one of them liked books, one liked pretty scrapbooks, and one liked the same series she did. It also helped that one of them had a hilariously adorable sister.

So in five steps, Aaloka had accomplished everything a genius would never do- Trial and error, and a great load of messing up. Terribly.

But did it matter to her?

No. That was a problem for future Aaloka.

27. Things the old man knows

The old man looks up at the house his grandchildren pointed to. "Tell us Grandfather." The oldest pleaded. The other three nodded in unison, going along with her lead.

He wasn't exactly their grandfather, but in a town full of young, clear-skinned, and strong people, it was rare to find someone as old and wrinkly as him. So, the kids had begun calling him 'Grandfather' and he'd grown rather attached to them too.

That evening he'd decided to abandon his usual spot on his rocking chair in the little garden house and take a walk around the quiet city in the East continent.

It was a pleasant place to live, set in the mountains with neat little houses with red tiled roofs, strings of pine trees across the woods, little fountains adorning the streets, and laughter of children echoing all around. It was far from the environment he was used to, but he liked it all the same.

As he thought about this, he'd bumped into the kids playing a game of pretend, where they liked to think they were brave soldiers fighting for the beloved East continent. It triggered a memory; one he pushed back a long time ago.

As soon as they saw him, they rushed to his side, bombarding him with countless questions, their eyes shining and hungry for answers.

The youngest pointed towards the large house to the very edge of the small city. "Grandfather," She asked, perched on his lap, eyes wide. "What's the story behind the ghost house?"

They called it the Ghost House because no one had lived there in over seventy years. It was large, with a blue tiled roof, which was very unusual in their little city indeed, and had broken doors and windows, vines creeping along the cracked glass. The wooden porch was lined with a thick layer of dust, and he'd imagined, no, remembered distinctly that the interior was the same. Antique wooden furniture, huge, towering bookshelves, and lots of dust. There was a rather ominous feel to the house, as if someone, something still lurked there. That fact alone had made the adults weary of the place and had told the children stories to keep them away from the house, and from potential harm.

"And what makes you think there's a story behind that house? It could very well be an ordinary house."

"Because grandfather, every house always has a story."

His eyes widened. *Every house had a story.* These kids sure had a habit of reminding him about old things. He decided to play along for the minute, simply to amuse himself.

"Ah but it's not a very interesting story. I could tell you one of princesses and dragons instead."

They protested immediately and he held back an amused chuckle. Children really had a way of making him feel warm inside.

"Please tell us Grandfather." The oldest pleaded.

He gave in. How could he not? He was not going to live very long as it was. Best he passed on what he knew, what he'd seen, so that knowledge would never die. This would be their little secret, unknown to the rest of the world, but it wouldn't die. Like a tiny flame it would be passed on, like a secret that never fades away. So, pulling out a tiny dairy from his coat pocket, he begins.

"Alright. Listen carefully. The story behind that house is a long one. It tells the tale of four young people, perhaps a little older than you lot. It is the tale of their show, to which I was a mere spectator."

28. And for what?

On 14th August 1947
A new country is born
On 15th August 1947
Bharat's shackles are torn
Smiles on every face
Jai hind! Fills the air
"For all, there is a place!"
"No matter what their race!"
But what is the reality?
Screams of terror
Cries of agony
Bloodstained gloomy weather
The people are puppets
The leaders, their masters
Look! Another one has kicked the bucket
It's worse than a natural disaster
Prayers have fallen on deaf ears
A united country split in two
So far away, yet so near
And the people cry- what do we do?
There is no right or wrong
Only Hindu and Muslim, nothing else
The weak run, as do the strong

Democracy cannot be heard over their yells.

It's another young girl assaulted,

Another young boy beheaded

Another family dead

Millions more on their deathbed.

And what to the leaders do?

Nothing, nothing at all

Because they too,

Are powerless in this brawl.

It's now 1999,

A look into time ahead,

Perhaps all is fine

Oh but this snake's skin has not been shed

The two countries continue to fight

Year after year, war after war

Every time the future seems bright

One makes a mistake and there's an uproar.

Deep dark blood and dust

Creeps upon the lush green city

Kargil's beauty has begun to rust

Oh what a pity

"Will this ever stop?"

Is all we ever ask

"Which country will come on top?"

Seems to be their only task.

29. We didn't ask.

The timid student takes a deep breath. The judge looks at him expectently, as does the rest of the audience.

He adjusts his glasses, his hands shaking.

'This one's for you, miss' He thinks solemly, and with a deep breath, he begins.

"I despise teachers people adore.

Because I adore them too.

They do everything so differntly, as if what people say won't matter to them.

I yearn to be like such a teacher one day.

And yet... Yet-

I wish people like them cease to exist

People like them, see, light up every dark and dingy room they're put in. They're the suns of the dull classroom solar system.

And we, we're the stars. The stars cannot shine without the sun. But stars collide. Stars get destroyed often. The sun can never destruct. Not for a while, anyway.

And the scientists that name these stars don't like the sun. They like to believe they are the reason the stars can shine so bright.

They don't think the sun letting it's light fall upon the stars is a good idea. But the sun does so anyway, because it is hopelessly selfless when it comes to it's stars.

And slowly, the stars are divided. To shine for the sun, who provides them the light, or to the scientists, who make them known?

They clash, they collide, they die.

Such people are blessings to society that are turned into curses.

They didn't deserve that.

But neither did we.

In short, don't help people like us. We're not worth your pain, your effort, your tears and your blood. We will adore you, shower you with our admiration, and turn our backs on you like the spoilt brats we are the second we're offered a less risky choice.

We can't do the right thing, and we're sorry.

We're so very sorry Miss.

He knows the tears are streaming down his eyes, and hears the horrified gasps of the crowd, but he doesn't care.

He feels the rough hands grab his arms and pull him back, but he feels nothing.

He deserves it, he thinks, as his vision dissolves into nothingness.

30. Don't eat yellow snow

I've never been very fond of people,
Even as a little child of maybe three,
So I suppose it's only natural,
That very few friends come to surround me.
I talk to a great many students at school,
A great many children at home,
But not a single one of them I shall take,
With me as a companion with whom I can roam.
And so the years passed by in this manner,
Where I had friends but none that feel true,
Until a fine day I meet a peculiar group,
Who start a chapter warm and new.
Sure they can be strange at times,
Saying things I do not understand much,
Cracking jokes I can't grasp humour in,
Calling me sweet little names that make my heart rush
But one thing's for sure,
And I can say it with pride,
They have my back,
And I'll always be by their side.
So here's a tribute to you all,
From your dear "princess" to you,

And with that I leave this here,
To leave now is my cue.

www.ingramcontent.com/pod-product-compliance
Lightning Source LLC
Chambersburg PA
CBHW031648170726
47990CB00019B/2894